W9-AOL-529

Twink's Magic Carpet Ride

by Jean Lewis
illustrated by David Gantz

A GOLDEN BOOK • NEW YORK
Western Publishing Company, Inc.
Racine, Wisconsin 53404

 Library of Congress Catalog Card Number: 84-73246 ISBN 0-307-16006-8
ISBN 0-307-66006-0 (lib. bdg.) A B C D E F G H I J

"Here she comes!" squealed Twink, bouncing up and down in excitement.

Twink and the Color Kids were welcoming Rainbow Brite home from an emergency trip to Bluegrass Country. A heat wave had scorched all the grass. But a shower of Star Sprinkles from Rainbow's pouch had soon brought the color back.

"Look at that!" exclaimed Red Butler as Rainbow's horse, Starlite, made a perfect landing on the grass from the arc of the rainbow.

"Isn't he graceful," said LaLa Orange as Rainbow jumped from Starlite's back.

Everybody crowded around to greet Rainbow. Everybody but Twink. He had bounced so high he got caught in a vine growing over the door to the Color Castle.

"Help!" he cried. "Please get me down!"

Buddy Blue plucked Twink off the vine and the grateful little sprite rushed over to welcome Rainbow Brite.

Twink heard Rainbow say, "Thank you for another smooth, safe flight, Starlite." She patted his neck.

"You're very welcome," answered Starlite. Then he began nibbling his favorite treat, the honey-sweet clover growing around the Color Castle.

Rainbow gave Twink a big hug. "I missed you," she said, handing him her pouch of Star Sprinkles to carry.

Twink beamed proudly, bouncing along beside her. Then he remembered the white daisies he had planted for Rainbow.

"Come out to the garden, Rainbow. I have a surprise for you," he said.

Meanwhile, down in The Pits, Murky Dismal and his sidekick, Lurky, sat hunched over a box bristling with wires.

"Static!" snorted Murky. "Can't you get anything but static?" As he hit the homemade TV, Lurky jumped up.

"Wait, boss, something's coming in on the Color Castle wavelength through our 'bug' in the garden."

"Sounds like a horse chewing," growled Murky as Starlite flickered onto the small screen.

"It is a horse chewing!" said Lurky. "Isn't that..."

"Shut up!" hissed Murky. "I want to hear what that brat's horse says."

"He's near our 'bug,' isn't he, boss?" snickered Lurky, pointing to a small microphone painted to look like a bee.

The two villains listened eagerly. Just then, they saw Rainbow Brite and Twink appear on the screen.

Rainbow and Twink came into the garden just in time to see the last fluffy white flower disappear into Starlite's mouth.

"Umm, de-licious!" said Starlite. "This clover has a special zip to it today!" And he tossed his rainbow mane.

"That zip is my daisies!" wailed Twink.

"Oh, dear, I am sorry, Twink," said Starlite. Then he flew off to Prism Pond. He needed a cool drink to wash down the clover—and the daisies.

Rainbow tried to comfort Twink. “Starlite didn't know he was eating your daisies,” she said.

But Twink could not be comforted. He remembered how hard he had worked to grow the daisies especially for Rainbow. He was angry with Starlite.

"Try not to think about it, Twink," said Rainbow as she went inside the Color Castle.

Twink began to water his flowerless daisy plants. "Everybody thinks Starlite's so graceful. I'd be graceful, too, if I could fly across a rainbow," he said to himself.

"So he wants to fly, does he?" said Murky. "We'll help him fly and the 'Rainbow Brat,' too—right into the cages we've got waiting for them down in the dungeon!"

Then Murky sent Lurky to the basement for four big metal clothespins, a small rug, and a giant magnet.

While Lurky rounded up the things, Murky opened his disguise trunk. He put on a flowing robe, a turban, and a long, white cotton beard. He looked like a magician.

"Behold!" he cackled. "Murko the Magnificent!"

"I'd never know it was you, boss," said Lurky, back from the basement.

"And now," said Murky, "I'll pack my bag of magic tricks!" He clipped the clothespins to one end of the rug and stuffed it in the bag, along with a cracked crystal ball.

"Bring the magnet and our walkie-talkies," he ordered, heading outside.

Lurky couldn't understand how Murky was going to make Twink fly, but he knew better than to ask questions.

Murky drove off in the Grunge Buggy, leaving behind a cloud of dust. Lurky peered through a powerful telescope aimed at the castle gardens and Twink.

He repeated Murky's instructions. "Keep your eye on the sprite, keep your ear to the walkie-talkie, and when I tell you, point the big magnet at the rug."

After hiding the Grunge Buggy in the bushes, Murky walked up to Twink.

In a high, quavery voice he said, "Murko the Magnificent can see your future in this crystal ball." He pulled it out of his bag with a flourish, keeping the crack hidden.

Twink put down his watering can. "What do you see?"

Murky peered into the crystal ball. "I see you flying," he said. "Ah, how graceful you are."

"Are you sure it's me?" asked Twink, trying to see.

"It's you, all right—flying on a magic carpet. One just like this!" And the wily magician unzipped his bag and whipped out the small rug. Murky and Twink both sneezed as dust flew from it.

Before he knew what was happening, Twink found himself seated on the carpet, waiting for lift-off.

Murky waved frantically at Lurky. "Murko to Lurky," he hissed into his walkie-talkie.

Through the telescope, Lurky watched Murky's amazing antics. Then he remembered to switch on his walkie-talkie.

"Magnet, dummy! Magnet!" crackled Murky's angry voice.

As soon as Lurky pointed the magnet at the metal clothespins, the rug lifted off the grass.

Twink let out a squeal of delight. "I'm flying! I'm flying!" he cried.

And so he was, six feet above the petunias!

When Twink called out that he wanted to land, Murky ducked behind a tree to signal Lurky to lower the magnet.

Twink made a bumpy landing on some rocks.

"Will the magic carpet hold two?" Twink asked.

"Of course," purred Murky.

Twink ran into the Color Castle to get Rainbow, and Murky hurried back to his Grunge Buggy.

"Fly right into my cages, 'Rainbow Brat' and Twink! I'll be waiting for you!" he cackled gleefully.

And he drove off to The Pits, still cackling.

KEEP OUT

"Twink, why do you want me to sit on this old rug with you?" asked Rainbow Brite.

"You'll see in a minute," answered Twink.

Suddenly, they were airborne.

"Twink!" Rainbow gasped. "When did you learn to fly?"

Twink beamed as they soared over Rainbow Land. He started to tell her about Murko when she grabbed his arm.

"Look, we're headed for The Pits," she screamed. "Turn around, quick!"

"I can't!" gasped Twink, struggling with the rug.

Straight ahead stood Lurky, pulling them to him with the magnet. Beside him, still in his magician's robes, Murky danced a jig.

"It's these metal clothespins," said Rainbow. "They're being pulled by Lurky's magnet." She unclipped one, and the rug dipped dangerously. Rainbow and Twink almost fell off. Then Rainbow remembered one of the things Twink did best.

"Twink," she said, "we can make a safe landing if you bounce. Each time I pull off a clothespin, bounce. That will steady the rug as we come down. Ready?"

Twink took a deep breath. "Ready," he said.

Twink bounced each time Rainbow unclipped a clothespin. They landed safely in a haystack.

I'm so proud of you!" said Rainbow, hugging Twink. "You're my hero!"

At The Pits, Murky yelled at Lurky, "It's all your fault!" Lurky got so flustered that he dropped the magnet on Murky's toe.

"Ouch!" howled Murky.

He howled so loud that Starlite heard him and came to see what had happened.

Rainbow told Starlite what Twink had done.

"Oh, my goodness," said Starlite. "How brave you were, Twink." Then Starlite opened his saddlebag. It was filled with daisy plants in bloom. "I felt so bad about eating your daisies that I went out and found you some new ones."

"Why thank you, Starlite!" said Twink, bouncing up and down.

Then Rainbow Brite and Twink climbed on Starlite's back for the flight along the rainbow, back to the Color Castle.

How nice, thought Twink, to leave the flying to Starlite!